TEN RULES

You ABSOLUTELY

MUST NOT BREAK

if You Want to Survive

THE SCHOOL BUS

by John Grandits

illustrated by Michael Allen Austin

 CLARION BOOKS | Houghton Mifflin Harcourt | Boston • New York | 2011

CLARION BOOKS
215 Park Avenue South, New York, New York 10003

Text copyright © 2011 by John Grandits
Illustrations copyright © 2011 by Michael Allen Austin

The illustrations were executed in acrylic paint.
The text was set in 15-point Billy Serif.
Design by Sharismar Rodriguez

Clarion Books is an imprint of Houghton Mifflin Harcourt Publishing Company.

www.hmhbooks.com

Library of Congress Cataloging-in-Publication Data is available.
LCCN: 2010024642
ISBN 978-0-618-78822-4

Manufactured in China

LEO 10 9 8 7 6 5 4 3 2 1

4500276142

For my "older" brother, James
—J.G.

For my "little" brother, Mark,
and a special thanks to the Gwinnet County Schools
transportation department
—M.A.A.

It was the first day of school, and my brother, James, was walking me to the corner where the school bus stopped. I'd never taken the bus before, and to be honest, I was a little nervous. But James was a school bus expert, and he'd promised to help me out.

"Pay attention, Kyle," he said.

"Don't walk on people's lawns. They don't like it when you do that."

I jumped to the middle of the sidewalk.

"And don't get to the bus stop too early! That's always a mistake."

I gulped. What *kind* of a mistake?

"But don't get there late, either. You'll get left behind."

My stomach turned over. In one of the nature shows I watch on TV, a young Canada goose got left behind when the flock flew south for the winter. I think it froze to death.

Too bad James wasn't taking the bus with me. Last year he rode the bus and Mom walked me to school. Then we moved. Now he gets to walk and *I* have to take the bus.

James had told me all about riding the bus. He said if you weren't careful, you could get laughed at or yelled at. You could get pushed around or even pounded. Big kids would steal your lunch and your money and even your football card collection! Sometimes I wondered if he was exaggerating a little. But if even half the stories were true, I was in trouble.

"So what am I supposed to do?" I'd asked him.

"Just think of what *I'd* do and try to act like me," James had said. "And always, *always* follow my rules." He called them the Ten Rules You Absolutely Must Not Break if You Want to Survive the School Bus.

I was going to follow every one of them. I didn't want to get pounded.

A couple of kids and their parents were already at the bus stop. There was a house with a fenced-in yard on the corner, and inside the yard there was a dog, barking like crazy. I couldn't see him, but he sounded like an arctic wolf that hadn't eaten all winter. The fence looked old and rotten.

"Better stay back," said James. "That dog sounds nuts."

"No lie," a big kid said to my brother. "I heard he ate a first-grader last year."

Everyone moved as far away from the fence as possible—even the grownups. But I had bigger things to worry about than some dumb wolf dog.

I had to ride the school bus all alone . . . by myself . . . surrounded by kids I didn't know.

Suddenly there it was: the school bus, charging right at me like a giant yellow rhinoceros! At the last second it jerked to a stop. The door swung open. Man, what was that smell? Last year's barf?

James waved and walked away. That's when the big kid pushed me aside, knocking my backpack to the ground. By the time I'd picked up all my stuff, everyone else was on the bus.

I climbed onboard. The driver was nasty-looking. "Hurry up, kid," she said. "I don't have all day, you know."

The first row of seats was empty, but I kept going because of . . .

RULE ONE:

Never sit in the first row.

The second row was filled—and the
third row, too. There were kids of every
size and shape and color on the bus,
and every one of them was staring at me.
I felt like a zebra at a lion party.
The fourth row was filled, the fifth,
the sixth. Oh no! Every seat was
taken except in the last row.
But I couldn't sit there
because of . . .

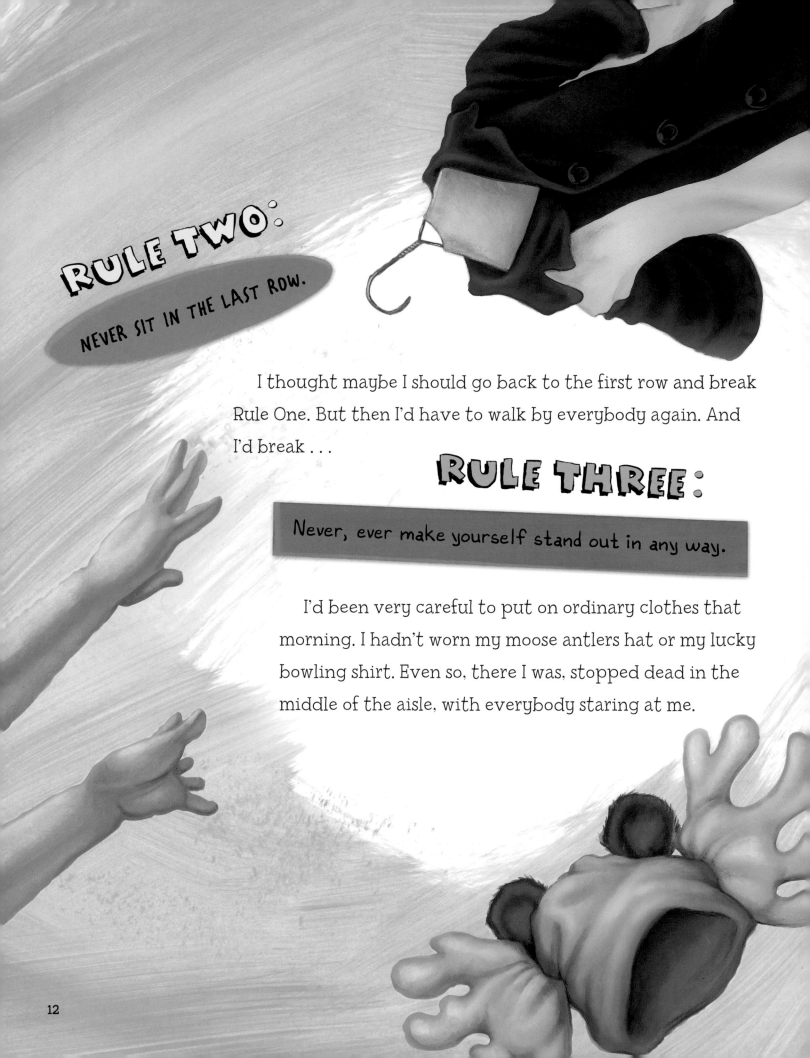

RULE TWO:

NEVER SIT IN THE LAST ROW.

I thought maybe I should go back to the first row and break Rule One. But then I'd have to walk by everybody again. And I'd break . . .

RULE THREE:

Never, ever make yourself stand out in any way.

I'd been very careful to put on ordinary clothes that morning. I hadn't worn my moose antlers hat or my lucky bowling shirt. Even so, there I was, stopped dead in the middle of the aisle, with everybody staring at me.

I walked to the last row and sat down. I had broken Rule Two and probably Rule Three because I didn't break Rule One. I stared at my shoes. The day was not starting out well.

There was a kid sitting in the window seat next to me. I could see legs and feet, jeans and sneakers. Was it a boy or a girl? I didn't want to be rude, but I was curious. I decided to take a peek—and immediately broke . . .

RULE FOUR:

NEVER MAKE EYE CONTACT.

"What are you looking at, dweeb?" It was the big kid from my stop, and he was glaring at me. Up close, he was the size of a grizzly bear. He must have been in the sixth grade, at least! Quickly, I looked away. My brother had told me that eye contact was very dangerous. If you looked at a kid wrong, he might lash out at you, like a cornered animal.

All of a sudden, the big kid's lunch bag fell off the seat!
Without thinking about what James would do, I picked it up.
That's when I remembered . . .

RULE FIVE:

NEVER TOUCH ANYONE'S STUFF.

"What are you doing with my lunch?" the big kid yelled.

"Nothing!" I said, tossing it into his lap. "It fell on the floor. I was just trying to help."

"Help yourself to my Twinkies, you mean!"

"No, honest. I just picked it up."

"Get out of this seat!" he growled. "You little kids are a pain!"

James would never have gotten into this mess because he wouldn't have broken . . .

RULE SIX:

Never talk to big kids.

"Big kids on the bus are bad," my brother had explained. "Never, *ever* talk to a big kid unless you're one yourself!" And I wasn't. So far the big kid had already yelled at me. Maybe he wasn't pounding me yet, but he might be planning to pound me later. I got up, crossed the aisle, and sat down.

There was a girl in the other half of the seat. "Don't pay any attention to him," she said. "I saw the whole thing. You didn't try to take his lunch."

"Yeah, but I shouldn't have touched his stuff," I said. "I guess I wasn't thinking." Which only proved that I *still* wasn't thinking, because I'd just broken . . .

RULE SEVEN:  NEVER TALK TO GIRLS.

James had told me that girls were even worse than big kids. They were as mean as snakes, they never stopped talking, and they hated sports. And if you were nice to them on the bus, they might want to sit with you at lunch.

Actually, that part didn't sound too bad to me. I wouldn't mind having someone to sit with at lunch. But my brother was the expert. And it was true: the girl hadn't stopped talking since I'd sat down. But I sort of stopped listening because the barf smell was getting to me and I had to concentrate on not adding to it.

Still, I snapped to attention when I heard her say, "That guy's not so tough, you know. One time I saw him run away from a squirrel! But he likes to pick on younger kids. He's a big bully."

Oh no! James had especially warned me to obey . . .

RULE EIGHT:

Never mess with the bully.

"Every bus has a bully," he'd said. "It could be a big kid or a little one, a boy or a girl. It doesn't matter. If you make the bully mad, your life will be miserable,"

I spent the rest of the bus ride imagining the bully beating me up all the way through grade school, high school, and college.

Finally, the bus screeched to a stop and I escaped. I found my classroom, met my teacher, and sat down with the other kids.

The rest of the day went OK, and one *nice* thing actually happened.
At recess I was watching a game of kickball, and I saw the talking girl
from the school bus. She was captain of one of the teams, and she was
really good! Anyway, while she was waiting for her turn to kick, she
came over and talked to me. And talked, and talked.

She told me that she took acting classes on Saturday, and yellow
was her favorite color. She knew a lot about chameleons, because she
had three of them. I was going to tell her about my ant farm, only she
didn't leave spaces for me to say anything.

Of course James *never* would have listened to a girl, but it wasn't
bad. In fact, the chameleon stuff was interesting, and she said I could
be on her kickball team tomorrow.

Finally, it was time to go home. But I couldn't find my bus. There were thousands of them. It was a herd of identical yellow rhinos. Which one was mine?

"Hey, new kid. Over here." It was the talking girl, hanging out of a bus window.

Yes! I'd found the bus—or at least it had found me. I hurried to get on, because of . . .

RULE NINE:

The driver frowned at me. "Sit down, kid," she said. "You're the last one onboard."

I could see that my brother was right about this rule. There were no seats left—except in the first row, right next to the big kid bully.

"Uh, hi," I said weakly, sliding into the seat. I didn't look him in the eye. Even so, I'd managed to break Rules One, Three, Six, Eight, and Nine in about thirty seconds. That must be a new world record. James would never approve, but I was too tired to care.

"Man, I hate the ride home on this bus."

Yikes! The big kid bully was talking to me! "Really?" I said carefully.

"Yeah, I always get a bad seat—like this one." He stared at me as if it were my fault. "And I hate where the bus stops."

"You mean, because of the dog?" I said.

The big kid bully grunted—which I took to mean yes.

"Yeah," I said. "What if it got loose? That would be real scary."

He nodded. "You'd think the bus driver could stop across the street. But nooooo!"

"Have you asked her?"

"Are you nuts? There are rules you have to follow when you ride the bus."

"Tell me about it," I said. And I remembered the last one on my brother's list . . .

RULE TEN:

"I never mess with the bus driver," said the big kid bully. "She's scarier than the dog on the corner." He smiled an evil sort of smile. Then he went on. "Why don't *you* ask her? You're a little kid. She probably won't yell at you . . . much."

I thought it over. I'd already broken every other rule. I might as well go for ten out of ten.

"Ms. School Bus Driver Lady?" I said, half standing to get her attention.

"Yeah? What? Sit down, kid!" she squawked. "No talking to the driver."

But I wasn't going to quit now. "There's a scary dog on the corner by our stop," I said. "Could you please drop us off on the other side of the street instead?"

"Oh, is that all?" she said. "No sweat, kid. Now sit down."

And that was it. I sat down.

The big kid bully looked impressed. "Wow! Good work!" he said. Then he caught himself and frowned. "Little kids get away with murder," he growled.

Maybe that was true, but I still felt brave. I'd broken every single one of my brother's rules. Even so, I hadn't gotten pounded—and I hadn't even barfed on the bus.

I walked on people's lawns all the way home.

James was waiting for me. He was so anxious to find out what had happened, he was jumping up and down like a spider monkey.

"How was the school bus?" he said.
"Where did you sit? Did you get pounded?
Who's the bully? Is the driver mean? You didn't
talk to any girls, did you? Was it terrible?"

"It was OK," I said. "I think I'll be all right. And I
learned something I never expected to learn."

"Oh, yeah?" he said. "What's that?"

I grinned at him and said . . .

Never, absolutely never, pay attention to your big brother's list of Ten Rules You Absolutely Must Not Break if You Want to Survive the School Bus!